THE LITTLE MERMAID

Manufactured in U.S.A.

8 7 6 5 4 3 2 1

ISBN: 0–7853–1028–2

Cover Illustration by Tim Huhn

Illustrations by Gary Torrisi

Contributing Writer: Dorothea Goldenberg

PUBLICATIONS INTERNATIONAL, LTD.

In the deepest part of the deep, blue ocean lived the old Sea King and his six mermaid daughters, along with the girls' grandmother. The Sea King had a great, long beard and ruled the ocean creatures with wisdom and kindness.

The youngest of the daughters, Princess Melody, had blue eyes, long blonde hair, and a lovely voice. All who heard it stopped, listened, and smiled. Nobody could resist the beauty of her voice.

Being a mermaid, Melody had a fish tail instead of legs. It helped her to swim underwater and play with her dolphin friends. Her best friend was a dolphin named Crystal.

Grandmother told many stories to the young mermaids as they laughed and combed their long hair. The mermaids made Grandmother tell their favorite stories over and over. Some of the best stories were about strange creatures who lived above the water and walked on legs. These creatures were called humans.

A mermaid was allowed to swim up to the surface on the day of her sixteenth birthday to see the humans. Melody could hardly wait!

On that day, Grandmother said to her, "Melody, today is a special day for you. You may swim up to see the humans. But you must not speak to them and you must return right away."

Melody was so excited. She darted up to the surface as quickly as she could fan her fish tail. Crystal followed close behind.

When Melody reached the ocean's surface, she saw a sailing ship anchored in the distance. She swam over and was amazed to see so many strange creatures—two-legged creatures—walking and dancing on the deck of the ship.

One of the creatures was a tall, handsome prince. She could tell he was a prince because he had a crown on his head, too. Melody sighed, "Oh I think I am in love with this wonderful man."

Just then, a bolt of lightning flashed, the sky turned black, and the waves grew taller. A storm snatched up the ship and broke it in two. The prince was hit on the head by the ship's mast and knocked overboard. He was too dazed to swim and began to sink beneath the waves.

Melody's crown fell as she rushed to catch the prince. She flipped her tail and carried him to the nearest shore. The prince's eyes were closed, so he did not see who had saved him. But he did hear her sing to him as she swam. Melody left the prince on the beach and swam back into the sea.

She waited near the shore to see who would come to help the prince. Before long, some children found him laying unconscious on the beach. They called their mother, who recognized him right away. She hurried to the palace to spread the news that the prince was alive. Everyone at the court was overjoyed. They thought the prince had died in the storm.

With tears in her eyes, Melody swam back to her sisters. "Oh how I want to be like human creatures."

"Grandmother, I can't forget my handsome prince. I must become a human so I can be with him," Melody said to her grandmother. Grandmother told Melody that only the Sea Witch could help her with a magic spell.

So Melody went to see the Sea Witch in her cavern guarded by sea dragons. The Sea Witch agreed to help Melody. She would give the mermaid human legs but Melody would have to give the Sea Witch her magnificent voice in exchange. Melody was unhappy, but she agreed to make the trade.

Handing Melody a silver cup with a magic drink, the Sea Witch said "Fish tail, fish tail, split in two. Give legs to this mermaid sweet and true." Melody felt her head spin as she sang good-bye.

When Melody opened her eyes, she was sitting on a sandy beach and her tail had been replaced with two beautiful, human legs. She realized that this was the beach where she had left the prince. Crystal swam near the shore, looking at her friend sadly.

The prince was walking on the beach that day. He saw her and came over. "Who are you? Where do you come from?" he asked. Melody tried to answer, but her voice was gone. All she could do was gesture with her hands.

The prince told her, "Never mind. My name is Prince Kyle. Don't worry, you can come back to the palace and I will take care of you."

He brought her to his home and was kind to her. Still, he longed to meet the lady with the beautiful voice who had saved his life.

Melody and Prince Kyle saw each other every day. They would take long walks on the beach and sometimes go sailing on the prince's boat. Melody loved to just sit and look at her prince.

Since she lost her beautiful voice, Melody could not speak or sing. She learned to use gestures to tell Prince Kyle what she wanted to say. The prince was enchanted by the graceful gestures Melody would make with her hands.

The days and nights were filled with laughter. Prince Kyle made sure that everyone in the palace treated Melody with kindness because she was his best friend.

While Melody was happy with her legs and her prince, the Sea Witch was unhappy with her new voice. The crystal ball she used to plan all of her magic spells was empty—it had no future to show her.

Now that her voice was sweet and soothing, the fish and creatures of the ocean no longer feared the Sea Witch. Instead, they swam around her cave playing tag with the sea dragon guards. Nobody took the Sea Witch seriously. Her sweet and beautiful voice canceled the wicked spells that she tried to cast.

Finally, she said, "This cannot go on! I must get my own fearful voice back."

One morning Melody and Prince Kyle were sailing on the prince's boat. Melody heard the Sea Witch singing, "Melody, Melody, take back your sweet voice. You may keep your legs, but return my fearful voice."

Melody wanted to answer the Sea Witch. She opened her mouth and, to everyone's surprise, out poured a beautiful, sweet song. The prince was surprised, but he recognized Melody as the lady who had saved him. He was so filled with love that he asked her to marry him right away.

The wedding was held on the deck of the ship, so that the Sea King, Grandmother, Melody's mermaid sisters, and all her other sea friends could watch.

After the wedding Princess Melody and Prince Kyle sailed away to the prince's land. But they built a palace by the sea so that Melody could be near her family and her sea friends. There, they lived long and happily together. Melody was always glad she had exchanged her fish tail for human legs, and Prince Kyle never tired of listening to her sing.